MONSTER PET!

For Celia
C. M.

For Digby
A. McA.

Margaret K. McElderry Books

An imprint of Simon & Schuster Children's Publishing Division

1230 Avenue of the Americas, New York, New York 10020

Text copyright © 2005 by Angela McAllister

Illustrations copyright © 2005 by Charlotte Middleton

First published in Great Britain in 2005 by Simon & Schuster UK Ltd.

First U.S. edition, 2005

The text for this book is set in Egg Cream.

The illustrations for this book are rendered in collage.

Manufactured in China

2 4 6 8 10 9 7 5 3 1

CIP data for this book is available from the Library of Congress.

ISBN 1-4169-0371-2

MONSTER PET!

Angela McAllister and Charlotte Middleton

Margaret K. McElderry Books • NEW YORK   LONDON   TORONTO   SYDNEY

Jackson was always asking his
mom and dad to get him a pet.
"I want a pet. I have to have a pet.
I neeeed a pet. Everyone has a
pet," said Jackson.
 "Pleeeease?"

"Get a worm out of the garden," said Dad.

"Why not bring home the class rabbit
for the weekend?" suggested Mom.

"**No!**" said Jackson.

"I don't want a worm or a weekend rabbit. I want a pet that's **big** and all mine. It's got to be **wild** and **exciting!**"

Dad bought Jackson a hamster.

"He's all yours, so take care of him."

"You must promise to give him plenty of food," said Mom, "and fresh water and exercise every day. And the hamster's cage must be cleaned out on Saturdays."

"I promise," said Jackson with a grudging look.

Jackson named his pet "Monster." Jackson tried to train Monster to fetch a stick, but Monster wouldn't budge.

Jackson tried to teach Monster to climb a tree, but Monster just sat there.

Jackson even showed Monster how to roar,

but Monster buried himself in his bed and wouldn't come out, not even for a bone.

On Saturday, Jackson forgot to clean out Monster's cage.

Then he forgot to change his water.

By the end of the week Jackson had enough pocket money to buy an old skateboard at the school fair, and he forgot to feed Monster altogether.

Down in the
shed Monster
got bored
and lonely.

He started to
feel hungry.

Up in his room
Jackson got ready
for bed.

Monster nibbled the latch of
his cage, pushed open the door,
and jumped into the bag of
hamster food.

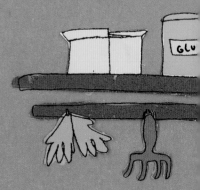

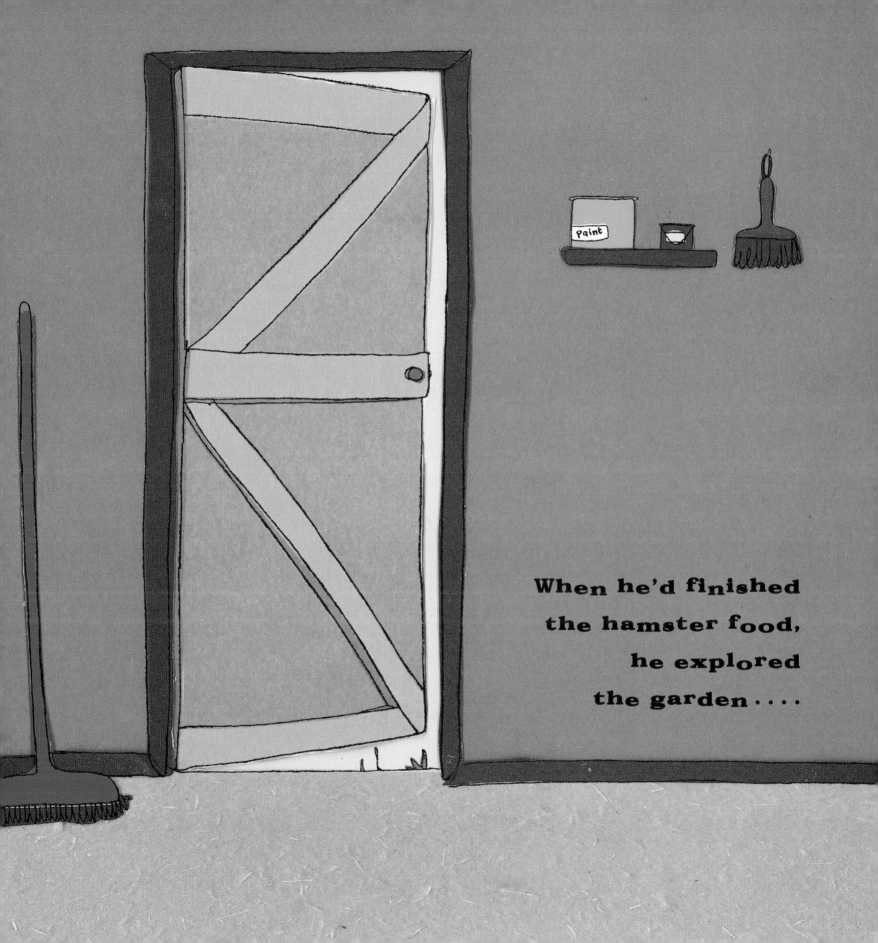

When he'd finished
the hamster food,
he explored
the garden....

Jackson, who was busy doing skateboard stunts in the back garden, didn't even notice Monster growing **big,** and **wild,** and **exciting...**

...until they both noticed each other.

"**WOW!**" said Jackson. "That's the sort of pet I want!"

"Oh, dear," sighed Mom. "Now, promise you'll look after him. He needs plenty of food and fresh water and exercise every day, and he must be cleaned on Saturdays."

"I promise!" said Monster.

Monster took Jackson to his shed. Monster tried
to teach Jackson to store food in his cheeks.
Monster tried to teach him to run around in a wheel.

Monster even showed Jackson how to build a nest,
but Jackson climbed into a big flowerpot and
wouldn't come out, not even for a bone.

Monster forgot to clean Jackson.
Monster forgot to change Jackson's
water or give him fresh bedding.
Before long, Monster found the
skateboard and forgot about
Jackson altogether.

Down in the
shed Jackson got
bored and lonely.

He started to
feel hungry.
Then he heard
a voice.

"Breakfast!" called Mom.
Jackson pushed open the door
of Monster's shed and . . .

...fell out of bed!

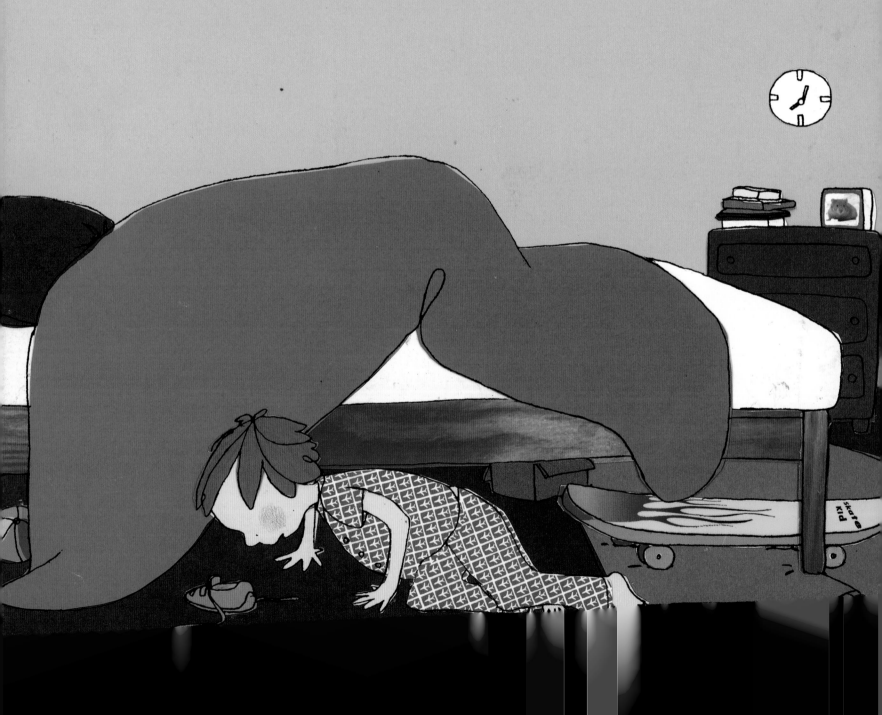

He rushed downstairs
but didn't stop for breakfast.

Jackson ran down
to the shed.

He picked up Monster and gave him
a handful of food. "From now on I'm
going to call you Fluffy," he said.
Fluffy looked up at Jackson and gave
a small, contented squeak.